Uniquely Backwards

Jane Brown

To order additional copies of this book, contact:
Xlibris
844-714-8691
www.Xlibris.com
Orders@Xlibris.com

ISBN: Softcover   979-8-3694-0454-6
         EBook   979-8-3694-0453-9
Library of Congress Control Number: 2023914266
Print information available on the last page

Rev. date: 07/31/2023

Uniquely Backwards

Famous Dyslexics

What they remember about school

He told me that his teachers reported that . . . he was mentally slow, unsociable, and a drift forever in his foolist dreams.

— Hans Albert Einstein, on his father, Albert Einstein

You should prefer a good scientist without literary abilities than a literate one without scientific skills.

— Leonardo da Vinci

My teachers say I'm addled . . . my father thought I was stupid, and I almost decided I must be a dunce.

— Thomas Edison

I never read in school. I got really bad grade – D's and F's and C's in some classes, and A's and B's in other classes. In the second week of the 11th grade, I just quit. When I was in school, it was really difficult. Almost everything I learned, I had to learn by listening. My report cards always said that I was not living up to my potential.

— Cher

The looks, the stares, the giggles. . . I wanted to show everybody that I could do better and also that I could read.

My problem was reading very slowly. My parents said "Take as long as you need. As long as you're going to read, just keep at it."

We didn't know about learning disabilities back then.

— Roger Wilkins
Head of the Pulitzer Prize Board

I am, myself, a very poor visualizer and find that I can seldom call to mind even a single letter of the alphabet in purely retinal terms. I must trace the letter by running my mental eye over its contour in order that the image of it shall leave any distinctness at all.

— William James

Psychologist and Philosopher

I was one of the 'puzzle children' myself – a dyslexic . . . and I still have a hard time reading today. Accept the fact that you have a problem. Refuse to feel sorry for yourself. You have a challenge; never quit!

— Nelson Rockefeller

Reference: https://www.dys-add.com/backiss.html#famous retrieved April 14th, 2007

This book is dedicated to all the students who have warmed my heart and inspired me with their ability to learn if I but find the means to teach them.

You say do it this way.

I wonder why I can't do it like this.

You say it is law.

I wonder whose.

Stay.

Creative Writing Example

Last Night I Went out to star

Belt. Orions And The Star Gaze I Saw the Big Dipper Little Dipper to star

You say think outside the box.

I realize for the first time
that I was never in and
hope no one notices.

Creative Writing

I am enjoying this assignment. i wish i could think outside the box all the time

WELCOME
SECOND
GRADE

In this job, you say,
one must be flexible.

I would like to borrow some concrete.

I'm told I believe in the kids.

I thank God someone believed in me.

11

Printed in the United States
by Baker & Taylor Publisher Services